Author's Note

This novella was written as a response to what I perceived as gross negligent appropriation of real-world tragedies.

Over the course of the 2010s, the West developed a growing interest in Aokigahara Forest—Japan's infamous "suicide forest" near Mt. Fuji. This began as innocent (if slightly morbid) fascination, but eventually became exploitation. Several horror movies, books, and games emerged set in the forest, and virtually none of them had anything meaningful to say about suicide, mental illness, or trauma.

This is my attempt at elevating this setting and giving it something meaningful to say. The Adrienne Forest State Park in New Hampshire is a fictitious location based on Aokigahara.

Come Forth in Thaw

COME FORTH IN THAW

A Novella

Jayson Robert Ducharme

Come Forth in Thaw

I.

Apropos of the Leaves

Come Forth in Thaw

An observation platform was coming up—a small parking lot jutting out of the mountainside. Along the iron railing that lined the edge of the platform were wooden benches and small telescopes that you could use at the cost of a quarter. After three hours and sixty miles, Ellie decided that here would be a good place to pull over. She hadn't stopped driving since she crossed the state border and her knees were aching.

The car slowed and she parked on the platform, sitting for several moments, trying to organize her emotions and thoughts. For the first time since leaving Somerville, she took her phone out of her purse and looked at it. Eight missed calls and seven texts, all from Clancy. Guilt pierced her stomach—that morning she had snuck out while Clancy was asleep. She knew that he would never allow this, but it needed to be done.

Swallowing, she slipped her phone into her coat pocket and got out of the car. The October breeze was freezing. It felt more like it was the dead of winter than autumn. The air was like dozens of needles prickling her face. It felt good. It woke her up. She strolled up to the railing of the platform and observed the colorful reds, yellows and oranges that rose and fell with the shapes of the mountains. The Presidential Range—she had only seen it once before, many moons ago. They were set against a sky that was swallowed by gray, without a hint of blue to be seen.

It was strange. Being this far north did peculiar things to her head. She was used to the noise of people, crowds, sirens, construction, as well as buses and trains. Up here, it was silent. There was nobody. It was as if she were the only person on the planet, up here in these mountains.

Ellie closed her eyes and whispered: "I'm here. I'm coming for you."

Time to go. Ellie stepped away from the railing and made her way back to the car, her knees thanking her for the quick stretch. Just as she reached for the car door, her phone vibrated in her pocket and that tinge of guilt returned.

God damn it, Clancy. She dug her phone out. "Hi," she managed.

"Ellie, you gave me a heart attack." Clancy's voice was appropriately disheveled. "Come home right now."

"I can't, Clancy. He's here."

"Ellie! No, you just—"

"I know he's here, Clancy. All the evidence is there. I can't ignore it anymore."

"The police, Ellie."

"They've wasted our time. I can't sit around any longer waiting on them when I know exactly where Alan is and what he's going to do. I have to do this now."

"They're coming. You need to—"

"Goodbye, Clancy."

She hung up. For several seconds she stared at her phone, expecting him to call back. She shut it off and decided not turn it back on until she was through with what she needed to do here. Shaking her head, she got into her car. *I'm sorry, darling*, she thought. *I promise you, after all this is over, you'll thank me. You'll see. Everything will be better soon.*

Alan was missing. The police had done all they could trying to find him, but to no avail. In Ellie's opinion, Clancy was too reliant on the authorities, and lacked the agency that she knew she had. She knew exactly where Alan was, and she cursed herself every moment of this ride north for not acting earlier. Alan was a troubled teenager, and this wasn't his first time running away. He fled from Somerville and—Ellie knew—had come up to these mountains, to these forests, to do what she most feared.

The clues were in a notepaper journal she found in his bedroom the evening before. It was worn out, with bent edges and crumbled pages, obviously having seen much use. Within it, he wrote about his struggles with himself, his life, and his future.

That journal now sat in the passenger seat of her car, lingering in the corner of Ellie's eye as she drove. She had brought it with her on this trip, as a reminder to keep going. It seemed to whisper, "Look at me."

A shudder quivered through her, and she pulled to the side of the highway and put on her hazards. A compulsion came over her to look at the journal again—this window into her son's mind—one more time before she reached her destination.

She took it, opened it in her lap and began to thumb through it. There were stanzas of poetry about death and suffering. Drawings of the Grim Reaper and Dante's Inferno. Random outbursts of scrawled writing pleaded: "THIS IS NOT A CRY FOR HELP" and "I JUST WANT TO DIE" and "THE SADNESS WILL NEVER GO AWAY."

There was no way to pinpoint exactly when it all went wrong for her son. Growing up, Alan had been an active and cheery child. Clancy took him to Little League, and he climbed trees and played archeologist in the woods with a five-year-old neighborhood girl named Danielle.

By all accounts, Alan Jackson was an active, ambitious, and sometimes playfully rebellious young boy. Nothing seemed outwardly wrong with him, and there was no specific event in his life that would explain his sudden shift in mental health. Yet, for some reason, not long after his eighth birthday, Alan changed. And there was no telling why.

It was something Ellie noticed immediately. There was just something about Alan that seemed to "slow down." No longer did he seem enthusiastic about all the things he used to enjoy. He stopped playing outside and participating in ball games, and even Danielle's mother called, wondering where Alan had gone off to. He just changed. He started sitting by the window of his room, elbow propped on the still, staring outside with a blank expression on his face. Ellie would try to reach out to him, ask if he wanted to go to the park or get ice cream. Alan wouldn't even look at her and would just mumble, "No, it's okay".

The behavior worsened. Alan became alienated at school. A councilor called Ellie once asking if everything was all right at home, mentioning that Alan was spending time by himself every day during recess, not talking to the other kids or teachers. His grades slackened too. Sometimes Ellie had to drag him out of bed in the morning just to get him ready for the day.

It was baffling and frustrating, trying to understand what happened to her son. It was like he was no longer the little boy she had loved, but rather some sort of changeling taking the appearance and most basic behaviors of her son.

Many nights, Ellie cried to Clancy in bed over it. "Where did my son go?" she would say to him. "I want him back. It's not fair. What happened to him?"

Clancy would just run his fingers through her dark Latin hair and whisper, "I don't know. But I wish I did."

Ellie blamed herself, as if she were somehow responsible. Clancy repeatedly persuaded her to believe that she wasn't a failure, and that instead there may be something psychologically wrong with him. After many fights, Ellie agreed to have Alan see numerous specialists. He was given several tests and was prescribed countless different medications, all of which either had no effect on him or only made his behavior worse. In an act of desperation, Ellie and Clancy agreed to have Alan stay at McLean Hospital in Belmont for a time, with mixed results.

It felt hopeless. Every day, Ellie missed that bright smile on her son's face, and missed the way he used to point at the clouds and see all different shapes, calling one a duck and another a sailboat. She missed her son. If he left this world, he would be taking her with him. If only he knew just how foolish he was being. Ellie wanted to grab him, hold him and promise him that she would do everything she could to make things right. Anything. Just don't go.

Nine years had passed since that change in her boy. Alan was seventeen years old now, a senior at Somerville High

School, with no prospects of a future in either employment or higher education. Now he was missing, and the police wasted too much time trying to find him in all the wrong places. But Ellie knew where to look, and she had to get to him before it was too late.

The journal got darker as Ellie browsed further, culminating in detailed fantasies about Alan coming here to these mountains. Her heart wretched with each morbid and dismal depiction of loss and misery. It was the final page that had brought her here. The final page had a drawing and a newspaper article stapled to it.

The drawing was of the dark visage of a person standing within a forest. Shadowy bodies hung from the branches all around him, and the roots of the trees resembled claws beneath him, reaching up to grab him and pull him into the ground.

The newspaper article, faded yellow from age, had the headline: "BODY FOUND IN ADRIENNE FOREST – 39TH OF YEAR."

Ellie's knowledge of the Adrienne Forest State Park was vague—the sort of thing she had always known of or heard about in passing.

It was a popular public forest and mountain trail in the White Mountains, laying at the base of Mount Waumbek—an

Algonquin word for "Mountain with a Snowy Forehead." It was nestled west of the Presidential Range between the town of Jefferson and the township of Clarke's Purchase. It was seven thousand acres and operated by the New Hampshire Division of Parks and Recreation, and part of the larger White Mountain National Forest. Since the nineteenth century the park had been used for hiking, and in the 1930s it saw a brief stint as a ski resort that got shut down not long after World War II. There were rental cabins, as well as covered bridges and an old cable car that went to the summit of Mount Waumbek. Lake Franconia was located there as well, and visitors often kayaked and fished. It was also a popular place for weddings and was featured in numerous television programs.

By all accounts, the Adrienne Forest State Park was a painfully average destination in a state that was oversaturated with parks. The only unique thing about it was that roughly between thirty-five and fifty people on average entered the park to take their own lives annually. It was the most well-known suicide hotspot in northern New England. The amount of bodies found in the park over the years grew so excessive that official figures stopped being published around 2003. The park's most costly year had been 1999, which saw sixty-seven people commit suicide in the forest.

Every spring, the state police and the Division of Parks and Recreation meticulously combed over the Adrienne Forest for bodies. Some of the licenses on the deceased indicated that they had come from as far away as New York and Québec. The most popular methods to die in the park were either hanging from the trees, overdoses, or drowning in Lake Franconia.

It didn't make sense to Ellie. Driving all the way up to the middle of nowhere to end your life seemed like such a hassle when you could do it at home or someplace nearby. She supposed there was an allure to it, as if it was a romantic place to do something so intimate—in nature, at peace, and alone. There was privacy as well, with no distractions, far away from people. It was also more likely that a state trooper would be the one to find you, rather than a loved one.

People escape into nature to relax, to get away from the oppressive chaos of civilization. Perhaps coming here was a more peaceful way to do it. There was a meditative quality to being in nature, and to end your life in nature would be like returning to where you came from.

Yet, why Adrienne specifically and not the other state parks? What was it about Adrienne that was so attractive to people who held sadness in their hearts?

According to the dashboard clock, Ellie had been sitting in her car for a half hour. She closed the journal and set it back in the passenger seat. In all this time, no car had passed by her.

It's so damn creepy up here, she thought. *So alone. So cold. The opposite of Boston and Somerville.*

The weather had changed. The sky grew dark, like it was becoming late evening, even though it was just past noon. A fog had begun to roll in around her vehicle—thin at first, but quickly getting thicker—making the world appear like some lunar alien planet. Perhaps it was going to rain soon. It felt like it was going to snow instead.

I'm coming, Alan, she thought, turning off her hazards and pulling back onto the highway. *If only you knew how far I've come for you…*

Not much further now. A mile or two. The fog had worsened since she started driving again, and she could only see a few feet in front of her. She slowed her car down to a comfortable forty miles per hour and sat forward squinting. A sign appeared in the mist, emerging from the soupy white haze like a ghost ship at sea: ADRIENNE FOREST STATE PARK. Ellie took the next right and was off the highway.

The exit took her down a narrow stretch of road with both sides lined with thick forestry. The branches of trees reached over the street like arms tunneling off the sky. The sun could only be vaguely seen like the swollen glow of a lantern behind a dark gray veil.

A parking lot appeared. Ellie pulled in and killed the engine. She was here. This was it.

A backpack she had brought along sat on the floor of the passenger seat. Methodically, she took it up and dug through it. Within was a large flashlight, a compass, a foldout knife and extra gloves, along with a few other things. Also included was a heated blanket. Looking through these contents, one would have thought she were going camping. Morbidly, Ellie chuckled at the irony of it all. She slipped the backpack and gloves on.

The parking lot was empty save for two cars; her own and a white Sedan parked nearby. Ellie approached it. The paint on it was grimy from the weather, and dead leaves and pine needles blanketed it. After brushing some of the leaves away, Ellie peered through the passenger door window. An old newspaper sat in the passenger seat, as well as some dirty clothes. On the dashboard were faded photos of what she assumed were friends and family. The owner must have left their vehicle here, went into the forest and never came out. These, the things the dead leave behind.

An impulse came over her. She dug into the front of her coat and pulled out a small silver locket. It had been a gift from her bother Emmanuel during a baby shower at the old apartment in Quincy a few months before Alan was born. Within it was a small photograph of her son when he was eight years old, just before the darkness had come and taken him away. She admired the photo, then clutched the locket in her fist and slipped it down the front of her shirt.

The entrance to the park was at the edge of the lot. A long gate arm was down in front of it and a wooden booth greeted anyone who wanted to enter. Opposite of the booth was a wooden sign with large golden letters nailed to it that read: ADRIENNE FOREST STATE PARK CIRCA 1845 – BIENVENUE – CLARKE'S PURCHASE – JEFFERSON - RANDOLPH."

In smaller carved and painted letters below this, toneless in comparison to the greeting above it, was inscribed: "Your life is a precious gift given to you by your parents. Think of them and the rest of your family and friends. You do not have to suffer alone. Please call 1-800-273-8255. There is hope."

There were plastic cases nailed to the sign that had several brochures stacked within them. Ellie took one and opened it. It had a map featuring all the park trails, and arrows pointed out various attractions such as waterfalls, rivers, glacial formations, Lake Franconia, and bathrooms. She folded it up and slipped it into her coat.

Nobody was inside the booth. Strange. It was a Saturday afternoon and nobody was working. There should have been many other people here, and yet she was completely alone. To her knowledge the only time the park was closed was during the winter months.

Ellie crept beneath the barrier arm that separated the lot and the trail. Ahead was a covered bridge going over a creek. For several seconds Ellie stood, looking at that bridge, which looked like some ghostly omen in the mist. One foot went out in front of her, and then the other followed, and soon enough the covered bridge swallowed her.

The sounds of her boots *clunk-clunk*ing against the floorboards echoed all around her, mixing with the current of the running water below. The opening at the other end of the bridge drew nearer, becoming larger.

The Legend of Sleepy Hollow, Ellie thought. *If you cross the bridge, you're in the Horseman's territory…*

And then she was on the other side. The bridge was behind her. She was in the Adrienne Forest.

For some time Ellie went down the Main Trail, feeling as if she were going nowhere. In the fog, everything looked the same—the trees, bushes, everything—but she kept walking, knowing that she was going somewhere.

19

It was eerie. The forest was completely silent. There should have been birds calling, or rivers running, or twigs snapping in the distance from wildlife, but there was nothing but light steps of her own feet against dirt.

Her mind wandered. This was a place people came to die. Somewhere off this trail there were perhaps some unfound remains, hanging from a tree or inside of a tent or in a river. It wasn't a far-fetched idea. A decent amount of dead had found home here since the last police sweep in the spring…

Stop it, Ellie thought. *You won't find anything if you just stick to the trail. Focus.*

You won't find Alan sticking to the trail, either, another thought told her.

Instinctively she stopped, knelt, then took her backpack off and took the knife out. She wasn't sure why, but she felt safer having it in reach. She slipped the knife into her coat pocket, put the backpack on and resumed walking. *Alan, where are you in this big, crazy place?*

According to her map, she just needed to continue going up this Main Trail, and eventually she would meet a fork—one trail going east called the Lafayette Trail, and another going west called the Butte-de-Tahure Trail. The Winscott River was near these trails, and—

A sound was heard straight ahead. A bell—a small one, dinging, then going silent, then dinging again.

It appeared first as a dark shape in the thick wall of white ahead at the fork, then it grew features the closer Ellie got to it. The sight was so peculiar that for several seconds she stared at what was there, unsure if the fog was toying with her eyes or if what she was seeing was really there.

It was a tinker vendor's wagon. It was a sad, rickety looking thing with a few wooden shelves, two large steel wheels and handles to carry it by. A small bell hung loose and rusty over the wagon. A man stood nearby, leaning against a tree with a cigarette smoking away in his mouth.

Ellie halted, her eyes keen on the man. He waved casually, pulled himself off the tree and took a few steps towards her. "Bon après-midi," the man said.

Ellie backed away, her hand in her coat pocket, gripping her knife.

"Whoa now, lady. Hold on. I didn't mean to scare you." He plucked the cigarette from his mouth and snapped it away. "I know all this might be a bit strange to you."

"Who are you?"

Defensively, the man chuckled, and approached her with his hands out. When he was about two feet away, Ellie could make out his features better. "I don't mean any harm, miss."

A strange man. He looked to be middle aged and homeless. There were thick lines in his scruffy face, and his beard was graying black. His eyes were dark and set so deep into his face that they looked black. His nose was large and red, and when he spoke, it was with a funny accent. His voice was casual, no-nonsense, and hoarse.

"I asked you who you were. There's no need to come any closer," Ellie told him.

"I'm just a bumbling old tinker, collecting goods, is all."

He was smiling at her—at least, that's what it looked like. His teeth were rotting. He wore a heavy plaid coat with the hood up, covering his long hair and ratty cap. His jeans were faded and ripped, and his winter boots clunked heavily against the frozen ground with each step he took.

"Is that right?" Ellie challenged. "What are you doing here?"

"It's good business here. Lots of tourism. This is a popular state park, you know. It's not like I'm not allowed to be here or nothing."

Ellie pointed at the wagon. "All that stuff you've got. You're selling it?"

"Selling?" The man laughed, looked at his wagon, then back to Ellie. He stuffed his large rough hands into the front pockets of his coat. "Nah, mon ami. I don't sell. Not often, at least."

"Then how do you make your business?"

"Collecting, mostly." The Tinker grinned half toothlessly at her. "Wanna see?"

Cautiously, Ellie took her hand out of her pocket, leaving the knife, and approached the wagon. There were all sorts of knickknacks on the wooden shelves. Strangest of all was the fact that they were all kept inside little jars. Each jar contained a single item each; a golden button, a glistening ring, a weaved bracelet, a roll of undeveloped film, a transparent blue marble. It went on like that.

As Ellie browsed, the Tinker stood next to her, rolling a cigarette. "May I offer you a dart?" he said.

"I've never smoked before in my life."

The Tinker nodded, then finished rolling the cigarette. He slipped it into the seam of his mouth, popped a match to life with his thumbnail and lit it.

"You've got a lot of stuff here," Ellie said.

"I've been collecting these for some time now. Priceless, is what they are."

"And you don't sell anything?"

"Oh, but I do sell things. Just not what you see on this wagon." He held an arm out to the mementos on his shelves. "No, I could never give these away. No… they're mine. They'll always be mine. And if you want to help me out, I can sell you something priceless."

"Charging what?"

"Favors, mostly."

"And what could you possibly sell me?"

The Tinker looked at her squarely, took a drag of his cigarette. The stench of tobacco was so strong that Ellie's eyes stung. "The way I see it, you came here for a very specific reason. Is that right, mon chéri?"

"Yes."

"And what's your name, mademoiselle?"

"Eleanor. Eleanor Jackson."

"I see. Is that your maiden name?"

"No. I'm married."

"How old are you?"

"Twenty-nine."

The Tinker smiled. "You look a little old for twenty-nine."

"The years have not been kind to me."

"Uh-huh. What day is it today?"

"Saturday. October 13th. Why?"

"Well, you see, I've been in this forest for a while now. Sometimes I lose track of time. Let me take a wild guess: you're here because somebody important to you has come here to do something you don't want them to, is that right?"

"Yes. My son. He hasn't been right for some years now. He's been on medications, he's been hospitalized, anything you can think of. Nothing has worked. And I think he's finally—" Ellie voice cracked.

"Say no more." The Tinker plucked the cigarette from his mouth and studied the burning tip. "I tell you what, Mademoiselle Jackson. I'll strike a deal with you. I have a favor to ask. I need you to get me something for my wagon. If you get it, then I'll offer you some information that'll get you going in the right direction."

"You know where my son is," Ellie said, stepping forward. "Tell me."

"I never said I knew where your kid was, just what direction to point you in."

"Where is Alan, you son of a bitch!"

Ellie leapt forward, her hands out to grab him.

"Whoa lady!" The Tinker threw his arms out and hopped back. "Do not touch me!"

Ellie stopped, her arms in mid-reach.

The Tinker laughed and wagged a finger at her. "Trust me. You don't want to touch me. You don't."

"If I do this favor for you, will you promise me that you'll help me find my son?"

"Never said I'd help you find your son per-se, but I know where you could start. That journey—finding him—that's all yours. That's on you, mon ami."

"What do you need me to do? I can't waste any more time."

The Tinker finished off his cigarette and crushed it out against the heel of his boot. "I'm tired, Eleanor Jackson," he said, leaning up against a tree and crossing his arms. "Very tired. It's been a very busy season. This time of year usually is. I'd like to just kick back and relax for a bit. The only thing I ask is that you retrieve an eensy-weensy, tiny-winey little thing for me."

Ellie waited for him to finish.

"A butterfly. If you follow the Lafayette Trail, you'll come across the Winscott River. Go east down this river for some time, and you'll discover a baby blue butterfly hairpin. I need that piece of jewelry, Eleanor. You get it, and I'll help you out. Quid-pro-quo."

Ellie's eyebrows went flat. "That's it?"

"That's all I ask. Nothing more. Just follow the river east, and you'll find it."

"A small piece of jewelry in a big forest like this—how will I know where to look?"

"Trust me. You'll know."

Ellie and the Tinker leveled each other with their eyes. Ellie glared at him while the Tinker playfully grinned with that ugly smile.

"Well, get on with it." He dismissed her with a condescending hand gesture. "You're the one who's in a hurry here, lady. Aller! Aller!"

Ellie pointed a firm finger at him. "You'd better help me."

The Tinker placed a hand over his heart and held the other up. "Cross my heart and hope to die."

Ellie passed the Tinker, not giving him another look, and proceeded down the Lafayette Trail. As she went, she could hear him popping another match against his thumbnail.

After several paces, Ellie was again alone. The trail looped around a large rock and went downhill. Eventually she heard running water. Ellie rushed down the slope until she came upon a narrow river, its white foamy waters creasing between colorful rocks.

Ellie took out her compass and turned in a few directions until she knew she was facing east. To follow the river as the Tinker had instructed her, she would have to go off trail. She didn't like this. She looked over her shoulder at the direction she had come from, thinking about the strange man she had just met.

What's that guy's deal? she thought. *What's he hiding? He's got some ulterior motives…*

Carefully, she drew the knife from her pocket and opened the blade, now looking in the direction she needed to go. "Okay," she whispered. It wasn't like she was going to have any other help here.

Biting her tongue, Ellie wandered off trail, walking along the river and into the maw of the forest.

She stepped over tree roots, as well as mossy rocks and steep ledges. A few times she was convinced that she had already passed what she needed to find. Nerves started to overtake her. And then it materialized ahead in the mist. A bright green dome camper tent was pitched next to the river. In front of it was a small firepit made up of rocks and sticks, long since burned out. A small trash bag lay nearby filled with plastic wrappers and water bottles. Whoever was here hadn't been here for very long, and they had been neat and organized about their presence.

"Hello!" Ellie called out to the tent. No answer. She shuffled from one foot to the other, rubbing the tips of her fingers against her thumbs. She took a few steps towards the tent. "Hello!" she called again.

Still nothing. The curtain of the tent was zipped up. Ellie crept closer. "If there's anyone in there, say something right now."

Nothing. Ellie's mouth went dry, and she squatted down in front of the curtain. After a few moments of licking her lips and fighting herself, she reached out, pinched the zipper, then began to undo the curtain. The distinctive odor of vomit made itself known.

"Oh Christ." Ellie stood and stumbled away. *No, I can't do this*, she thought, putting her hand over her mouth.

The Tinker…

Fuck the Tinker.

What are you going to do without his help?

Ellie stood before the tent in the middle of this vast and miserable forest. Alan could be anywhere and she had no idea where to even begin looking for him. Her eyes set themselves on the tent again. She felt ill.

"Okay," she told herself.

Once again, she approached the tent, focusing on that half-opened curtain. Again she squatted before it and reached out for the zipper. This time, she undid the entire curtain. The stench inside was so vile that she turned her head away and took short breaths through her mouth.

Inside was dark. Ellie took out her flashlight and her trembling thumb pressed against the button. The face of a young girl appeared in the light, gray and still like a porcelain doll. Her empty eyes were half open, and there was dried vomit crusted around the edges of her mouth. More vomit was pooled into the pillow her head rested on.

One hand lay palm up by her side, the wrist slashed, and dried dark blood stained the white blanket on the ground. It looked as if she hadn't been dead for more than a day. The only color left in her was the purple bruising of uncirculated blood pooling in the bottommost parts of her body. *Late last night*, Ellie thought. *Perhaps very early this morning.*

Near her hand was a torn photograph. Ellie reached in and took the photo. Within it, the girl stood before what looked like a university. Whoever was in the photo with her had been torn away, and the only remaining thing left of that person was a single arm reaching around her shoulder.

In the girl's smooth brown hair was a jewel butterfly pin. Morosely, Ellie set the photograph in the girl's bloodied hand and took a moment to examine her face. This was the first time she had ever seen a dead body up close.

There was this strange perception of how death was "supposed" to look like. In movies, characters passed away on screen looking no different than somebody with their eyes closed. Funeral homes dressed up, did makeup on, and filled the deceased with embalming fluid to give them as lively and natural a look as possible. Even in the images of Christ, we see him on the cross, looking pure and untouched by the elements.

The real thing was far different. Like Rogozhin losing his faith upon seeing the Body of the Dead Christ in the Tomb, whatever perceptions Ellie may have had about the dead were shattered upon witnessing this. The only thing she kept thinking about was how awful it all was. To die like this, looking like this, smelling like this. The longer Ellie stared at the dead girl, the more she felt she could no longer take it once the initial morbid fascination passed.

Ellie snatched the butterfly pin from the girl's hair and staggered away. She leaned against a tree and wiped her face. *Please don't let me find you like this, Alan.*

Ellie pulled herself off the tree and looked at the pin in her hand. If she was to find Alan, the Tinker needed this. Ellie washed away whatever guilt she felt from what was essentially grave-robbing and instead focused on her determination. To find her son before he became what this young girl was now.

At the fork in the path, the Tinker sat perched on a low branch, kicking his legs playfully in the air beneath him. "Well?" he said.

Ellie lifted the butterfly pin up.

The Tinker clapped his hands together. "Oh, magnifique! Très bien!" He hopped off the branch and scurried up to her with his hands out like some beggar. "Give it here!"

Ellie held the pin back. "You'll help me?"

"Yes, yes! Of course! Just give it here! Drop it into my hands—remember, no touchies."

The pin fell into the Tinker's dirty, calloused hands and his fingers curled over it like a flytrap. "Very good," he said. He held the pin carefully between thumb and forefinger and drew a pair of thick framed glasses from the front of his coat and slipped them on. In a seemingly impossible feat, the Tinker managed to make himself look distinguished. He held the pin up, squinted as he turned it over front to back.

"Yes," he said, returning the glasses to his coat, "very good."

From a cabinet below the shelves of his wagon, the Tinker took out a small yellowing jar. With ease, he popped the cap off, dropped the pin inside, screwed the cap back on and set it on the top self among the other mementos.

Ellie approached him. "Tell me where I need to go to find my son. I did what you asked."

The Tinker nodded and rubbed the ball of his thumb against his rough chin. "Of course. I'm a man of my word. There are a few things I should explain before I send you on your way, Mademoiselle Jackson. Your son intends to take his own life, is that right?"

"Yes."

"A lot of people come here to do that. Interesting expression, yeah? 'Taking your own life.' From who? Once it's gone, it's not yours to take, and it certainly won't be yours to miss. I've been here for some time and I've come to learn a thing or two about this place and the people who come here."

"Why do they come here to do it? Why this park?"

"A place like this forest... it holds a lot of suffering in it. People who carry pain with them bring it here and leave it when they die. All that pain just gathers here, like a cauldron. The more suffering the forest gathers, the more influence it has over people who hold pain in their hearts. It may sound like a bunch of hokey henshit, but I think there's a lot of truth to that."

"What's your point?"

"Sorry," the Tinker smirked in embarrassment. "Didn't mean to soliloquize in front of you. My mind, she just wanders. But I suppose my point is that people come here to die. At least, those who are determined to die. It's a mental commitment. They come here, enter the forest, and they do their business straight up. No delays, no nothing."

Ellie's face went long. "What are you saying?"

"Don't jump to any conclusions—I'm getting to your son. What I'm saying is that while people come here to do what they came to do straight off... there are those who linger."

"Linger?"

"Correct. They want to die, but they are undecided. They haven't committed to the act. They were drawn here, but they're uncertain, scared and confused. It takes them a while to decide whether they want to do it or not."

"You're saying that my son is one of these non-committed cases?"

"Some of these non-committed types come in here knowing that the forest is big and that they'll be going off trail. Sometimes they'll bring a ribbon or some rope with them, and they'll tie it to trees to find their way out if they change their mind."

The Tinker pointed a long dirty finger down the Butte-de-Tahure Trail. "Go down this trail. Keep your eyes on the left. You'll find something familiar. Once you do, I think you'll be able to figure it out."

"Is that all?"

The Tinker took out some rolling paper, dripped tobacco into it and licked it shut. "For now. We'll meet again, Eleanor." He twisted the ends of the cigarette and slipped it into his mouth. "Be sure of that."

Ellie passed the Tinker, making her way towards the Butte-de-Tahure Trail. Before she was a few steps in, the Tinker's rough voice stopped her: "Say, Eleanor!"

He popped a match and lit his smoke, looking at Ellie with concern in his eyes. "One thing I forgot to mention. If it takes you longer than you expected to find what you're looking for here, then keep this in mind, okay? This place... well, like I said, it's experienced a lot of pain over the years. Just try not to hang around too long after the sun goes down."

Ellie said nothing. She proceeded down Butte-de-Tahure. The mist swallowed the Tinker behind her.

The trail went upwards, hugging narrow slopes of the mountain. This put strain on Ellie's ankles and knees as she went, but she ignored it and kept her eyes focused on her left, waiting for whatever this so-called familiar thing to appear.

After perhaps a mile, it did. It stood out in the white and gray world—a bright yellow rope tied around a tree. It was the same rope Clancy kept in the downstairs closet to tie around branches in the backyard during the winter to keep them from breaking under snow. Alan must have taken it with him.

It was tied loosely around the tree and was strung to another tree several feet off the trail, and then another. This created a makeshift trail leading into the forest. With her fingers caressing the rope as she went, Ellie followed it.

Five yards off trail appeared a clearing. Within stood a small rickety cabin that looked to have been in disuse for some time. The foundations of other cabins could be seen protruding from the ground like broken grave markers. This must have been an older resort area used many years ago for campers, but had been since abandoned.

Ellie approached the sole-surviving cabin. Its windows were cracked and musty, the walls decomposing. The roof had sunken in, allowing what little daylight there was to creep in. The front door was hanging off its hinges. When Ellie walked up to it, the odor of swampy wood and moss was prominent. With no effort, Ellie was able to push the door open and step in.

The remains of what looked like a table with wooden chairs sat on one side of the room near an old filthy refrigerator filled an old bird nests and leaves. Opposite of this was the rusty steel frame of a bed and the skeleton of an old mahogany dresser with no drawers. The busted remains of an alarm clock sat on top of the dresser with the shadowy imprints of what were once spade hands on its face.

Hanging over the bed, tied to a termite-embroidered ceiling rafter, was more yellow rope. It was done up in a noose—double looped, with three strong knots keeping the necklace together. It was a very well-done noose; strong and carefully made. A noose crafted with no mistakes in mind regarding its intended use.

The noose filled Ellie with both loathing and relief. Loathing from imagining her child being in such a thing and relief to see that he wasn't in it at all. He was still here somewhere. Like the Tinker had mentioned, Alan was one of those 'semi-committed' ones. There was still time to find him.

Desire and hope filled her heart. Ellie rushed out of the cabin. "Alan!" she called. "Where are you? I'm here! I'm here for you!"

The only response was her own echo.

Where the hell could he be? What if he got lost, wandered away?

No, Alan is a smart kid. He brought that rope from home and tied it around those trees specifically to find his way back here. If he wandered off, he would have found his way back.

Indecision ravished her. *Good Christ, what do I do? Do I go back to the trail and look for him? Is he on another trail, perhaps even going to the summit of the mountain? He wouldn't set all of this up just to abandon it, would he? Do I stay here and wait for him to come back? What if I go looking for him and he comes here while I'm gone to finish the job?*

It was all so overwhelming. Ellie went over to a large rock and sat down on it. She dug her locket out and caressed it with her thumb, looking deeply into the eyes of her son in the photo within. When her eyes came up from it, they found something that solidified her decision.

Nailed to a tree was a stuffed animal wolf wearing a tuxedo that Ellie bought Alan when he was six years old. It was withered and worn from years of use, as Alan had cuddled it every night until he was well into his teens. He always called him Mr. Wolf.

Mr. Wolf was nailed upside down by the hands and feet like some deranged version of da Vinci's *Vitruvian Man*. Ellie slipped the locket back down the front of her shirt and approached the anthropomorphized stuffed animal. His black beady eyes were set sadly in his dirty face. Why would Alan do this to a cherished toy from his boyhood? It was as if he were making a statement.

As morbid as it may seem, this could have been a positive sign. Alan was finding ways to express his emotions, putting off what he intended to do. He was wandering this forest, frustrated and angry. If he was going to hurt himself, then he wouldn't have bothered with such theatrics.

It grew dark. Ellie sat on the rock, waiting. Several times she got up and wandered around, calling out her child's name, waiting for an answer that never came. She had to continuously fight herself from leaving as time drew on with no sign of him, but fear of him coming back while she wasn't there kept her firmly in place.

Full night came, and with it, the cold. It was so cold that Ellie's face and hands went numb and her breath could be seen. Guided by her flashlight, Ellie went around collecting twigs and rocks to make herself a makeshift campfire pit. This was something she had learned from Clancy during their dating years. Having grown up in Merrimack Valley most her life, Ellie didn't know her face from her ass when it came to camping essentials until Clancy took her up to Vermont for a weekend. While up there, he taught her how to make a fire, among other things.

The worlds from which she and her husband came from couldn't have been more different. She was raised in a duplex with seven people—her brother, parents, uncles and grandparents. Home was a Dominican neighborhood on Union Street in Lawrence, Massachusetts. As Ellie started rubbing the sticks and dry leaves together, she reflected on that pothole-strewn street, always full of children riding bikes or playing basketball with Latin music dancing on the air.

Ellie's brother Emmanuel was four years older, and he had always been protective of her. If she got made fun of at Arlington Elementary, Emmanuel always challenged those who dared make such an offense to meet him in the parking lot. He pummeled a few punks back in those days, but he wasn't all aggression. There were many times where he took Ellie biking down the abandoned railroad tracks near the neighborhood to go fishing in the Merrimack River. Sometimes he'd be out all day picking flowers to bring home and give her. There really was no gift like having a loving older brother.

Sparks rose from the sticks, and a fire grew in the dry leaves. Ellie fanned the flames and blew on them. After she got married, Emmanuel moved somewhere out in Washington State. *Emmanuel*, she thought. *It's been so long since I've heard from you. I wonder what you're up to.*

Clancy was from a more affluent neighborhood in Methuen, the city next to Lawrence. He was an only child and grew up camping and hunting. He was always clean shaven and had a head of curly hair with a sharp nose—a nice man to look at. He wasn't handsome in any sort of traditional way, and that was what Ellie liked about him. He was the most exotic man she'd ever met. There was a gentleness to him that she didn't find in most men, who were always so territorial. This gentleness, Ellie figured, was what attracted her to him. When he offered to walk her to class and she declined, he didn't push. When he laughed at her jokes—which few men did—it was with an expressive giggle that she hadn't gotten sick of since.

They met while taking Statistics in Psychology at Northern Essex Community College. Their desks were on opposite sides of the classroom. One day when Ellie looked up from her notebook, she saw him catching a glance at her. Quickly, he looked away as soon as she noticed him, but she kept eyeing him until he looked back again and saw her looking.

The first time they ever actually spoke to each other was actually an embarrassing moment. After class, she made her way to the lobby. There was a short staircase leading down from the corridor to the lobby, and as she was about to make her descent, she noticed Clancy crossing the lobby towards her. Instantly nerves took hold, and she clutched her bag to her chest and pretended to not notice him. After two steps down, she slipped and caught herself on the handrail, but her bag took a tumble. All her books, papers and binders spilled out all over the floor.

Ellie could only imagine just how red her face had been. It was humiliating, and she kept her eyes on ceiling, unable to look at the boy coming towards her. When she finally gathered the courage to look, she saw him kneeling at the foot of the stairs, collecting all her books and paperwork, sticking it all back in her bag and clipping the buckles shut. He didn't give her any sort of mocking jeer. As he went up the steps with her bag, he merely gave her a quiet, knowing smile.

"It almost got away from you," he said.

Ellie laughed, rolled her eyes and took the bag. "Thanks."

"See you tomorrow." He passed her on the stairs and went down the hall.

Despite the disgrace, she felt assured. If there was any way to break the ice with a boy she had no idea how to approach, it might as well have gone like that. The following day she sat at the desk next to him and they chatted before class began. After that they began eating in the cafeteria together. After that, he took her to a movie, then they began going on nature walks.

The moment she knew she loved him was after three months of dating, when it rained in the middle of a hiking trip in the Berkshires. He took her by the hands and danced with her over the protruding rocks of a river. It was so scary and exciting, going with the rhythm as the rain poured down on them, trying to step on the right rocks or risk falling into the running water. At the end of the tango, he pulled her close, the two of them dripping wet, and he kissed her. Ellie told him that she loved him. Clancy said that he loved her too.

The fire comforted her. For the first time she felt at ease since she came here. Ahead she could see the dilapidated cabin, looking at her from within the dark, those dark windows resembling the frightened eyes of an animal. She rubbed her arms and rocked back and forth, trying to keep circulation going through her body.

Leaves rustled. Ellie looked over her shoulder at the dark curtain behind her. Silence, then rustling again. Leaves crunched and twigs snapped. *An animal, maybe a deer or moose?* She stood up and drew her knife from her pocket. "Who's out there?" she called. Instantly she regretted bringing attention to herself.

Whatever was out there ceased moving. Swallowing, Ellie sat back down, knife in hand. Whatever was out there was gone now. Just an animal.

Another sound came. Once again Ellie got up, gripping the knife so hard that her fist trembled. She could see nothing beyond the few feet of orange glow that the fire allowed.

A woman was whimpering in the woods and moving around. Ellie's mouth went dry. Her foot came up to kick out the fire, but the idea of being alone in the dark with whoever was out there was too terrible a thought to do it.

Trying not to panic, Ellie sleuthed to the cabin and shut the door. The door did not stay shut, so Ellie took the rotting dresser and dragged it over to the door and pinned it against it. Through the broken windows, Ellie could see the light from the fire outside, dancing against the stage of trees and night. She squatted in a corner near the bedframe, holding her knife in both hands.

More movement was heard outside. Frozen leaves crunched under footfalls. It ceased, was silent for several seconds, then resumed. A shadow passed against the fire's light, then vanished. Ellie held her breath, staring at the windows, wishing whatever was out there would go away.

The footsteps approached the front door. Knuckles rapped against it, the knocks dully echoing throughout the cabin. Ellie shut her eyes and covered her ears. *Go away*, she prayed. *Please go away.*

The rapping came again, and then silence. Then fists slammed against the door, trying to shove it open against the weight of the dresser. Ellie bit her lip so hard that she tasted blood. *I just want my son back*, she thought. *I don't know who you are or what you want but please, just go away. I can't help you.*

A woman sobbed behind the door, followed by a pained gurgling sound, and then the footfalls left the cabin. Again, it became silent.

Ellie opened her eyes. The door was slightly ajar, and the orange light of the fire crept into the cabin. She thanked the stars that she had pulled the dresser in front of the door. One half of her wanted to peek outside, and the other half told her to stay in the corner she had planted herself in.

Sleep didn't come to Ellie. She remained in that corner until the sad morning light seeped in through the broken ceiling. When it did, Ellie felt safe enough to get up, pull the dresser off the door and step outside.

The mist endured. The fire was nothing more than a few weak smoking embers now. A distinctive smell came to her as she approached the campfire, a mixture of iron and vomit. It was the same smell that had come from the dead girl's tent the day before. All around in the leaves and on the trees were smears of blood and droplets of vomit. On the front door of the cabin were maroon handprints.

As she kicked out whatever life there was in the fire, she found something. Upon the rock she had been sitting on the night before was a message, written in what looked like charcoal: BELLEVUE PASS. DON'T TELL TINKER.

Ellie squinted at this crude message. Was this written by her visitor, or…?

A bell sounded. The Tinker's wagon was coming. In a rush, Ellie looked around, grabbed a handful of leaves and spread them over the message on the rock. She turned just in time to see the Tinker coming into the clearing, dragging his wagon behind him. He set the wagon down and raised his arms up to stretch.

"Hell of a workout," he said.

Ellie stared at him with her hands in her pockets, looking like a kid trying to save face after doing something she shouldn't have.

"Not gonna say hi?" The Tinker sauntered up to her. "I see you found what you were looking for. Even made it through a night here too, huh? How'd you manage?"

"What the hell was that?" Ellie said.

"What was what?"

Ellie pointed at the blood smeared on the front door, and at the traces of vomit near the campfire. "Something came to me last night."

The Tinker gave her a knowing look.

"I want answers!" Ellie shouted.

"You already know damn well enough what was out there. I told you to watch yourself when the sun goes down, Mademoiselle Jackson. This place is not unlike any graveyard or tomb. The dead don't rest easy here. No, they struggle. All the more reason to find your son, yeah?"

"It's so awful."

"Yes, it is awful." The Tinker took a nail file from a drawer in his wagon and began casually running it against his fingertips. As he did this, Ellie saw that his fingernails were unnaturally long and yellow. "Suicide—the nature of it. It takes a lot of strength to do something like that, don't you think?"

"'Strength' is not a word I'd use."

"You know what's more awful though?" The Tinker looked at her with an excited expression. "Failed suicides. Those are substantially more terrible, aren't they? I've seen quite a few of them in my time here. A messed-up gunshot, even some hangings get botched too."

"Why do you think about all this? It's fucking morbid."

"You know what people think about after these failed suicides? They think about how much they want to live. The initial terror that precedes taking their own lives was supposed to end in death—after the initiation, that terror is carried over when what was supposed to kill them doesn't. They think to themselves, 'Please let somebody find me', or 'Please don't let me bleed to death out here'. It's funny, really. Why would you think these things when you yourself wanted it?"

"I don't understand it, Tinker. And I don't *want* to understand it."

"You know, I just remembered one of those failed suicides. A couple years back, this girl—Cassandra, I think her name was—she got married right here in this forest. A lot of people get married here, despite the park's reputation. There were tables with candles and a gorgeous marble ceremonial arch done up in flowers. Some months into the wedding, the groom turns out to be a serial abuser, and after years of slapping her around, he ditches her."

"Why are you telling me this?"

"The poor girl came back here, to the very place where she married this guy, then jumped off a cliff." He clapped his hands in the air. "Boom! It doesn't kill her though. She survives, all mangled against the rocks that broke her fall. Suddenly she doesn't wanna die anymore, and she lays there for three days screaming and crying for help. Those cries echoed all through these woods, but nobody heard them."

The Tinker turned to his wagon, took a jar with a wedding ring in it and held it up for Ellie to see. "See this? I snagged it off her not long after she finally croaked. By the time I got there the coyotes chewed her all up."

Ellie knew exactly what he was trying to do. He was playing head games with her—making her think that Alan was dying out there, putting anguishing images in her head. It was the perverse look he gave her as he told this yarn that bespoke his intentions.

"The point I'm trying to get at, Ellie"—the Tinker set the jar back on the shelf, ran his finger affectionately around the lid—"is that the lost souls who wander these woods don't wanna be dead anymore. But they are."

"He was here," Ellie said. "He made a noose, but he didn't go through with it. He's still contemplating it. Even if he doesn't hurt himself, it's dangerous out here by himself. He could fall or run into some wild animal. And the cold... good Christ, it was freezing last night. So much colder than I thought possible for October."

"I tell you what, Eleanor. For another favor, I could bring you one step closer to what you're looking for."

"Do I want to know what this favor is?"

"Depends on how badly you want to see your kid again. Theoretically."

"What is it? More grave robbing?"

The Tinker held his hand out to Ellie. "You got something I need. Your locket, mon chéri." He rubbed his fingertips against his thumb. "I need that locket from you."

Ellie took the locket from the front of her shirt and clutched it in her palm. "No," she whispered.

A flash of anger crossed the Tinker's face. He took a step closer. "Ellie, you want to see your kid again, don't you?"

"You can't have my locket."

The Tinker's hand curled into a tight fist, and he tucked it into his pocket. "Suit yourself. That's entirely your decision. But know this: this search for your son is only yours headnow. You'll cave and come crawling back to me. They usually do." He spat a thick wad of phlegm into the leaves. "Au revoir, et bonne journée!"

He lifted his wagon and strolled out of the clearing, vanishing in the fog just as smoothly as he entered.

Once alone, Ellie brushed the leaves off the rock, looking at the charcoal message: BELLEVUE PASS. DON'T TELL TINKER. She unfolded her map and scanned it until the name leapt out at her. Further up Butte-de-Tahure was another trail, simply called Summit Trail. This lead straight to the top of

Mount Waumbek. Near the summit was a mountain pass—
Bellevue Pass.

Guess I'm going on a hike today, Ellie thought without humor.
She folded up her map and stuffed it into her coat.

The trail was steep and rocky. Many times Ellie had to stop
and take a seat to catch her breath. Each time she did this, it
became increasingly difficult to get back up and keep going.
Sleep deprivation was taking its toll on her. After each rest, she
slapped herself in the face a few times, then managed to get up
and force herself up the mountain, inching her way closer to the
top.

As she ascended, the forest began to vanish. The trees
trickled out and the soil bled away to pure rock and granite. A
powerful wind had engulfed her, blowing through her clothes
and hair. On more than a few occasions she found her balance
on the ground difficult to control.

The summit of the mountain could be seen. Ellie stepped
onto Bellevue Pass, and she could look down the mountain at
the Adrienne Forest below, entrenched within a thick white
vapor with only the tops of the trees visible like tombstones.

Between the summit and the pass was a massive tree. Its
trunk was monstrous, like a giant's leg sprouting out from rock
and vanishing into the clouds above. Sprawling branches

resembling thick spiderwebs pressed against the white sky. Roots weaved themselves through the rocks from where Ellie stood to the base of the tree's trunk like pulsating veins. Human parts were rooted into its bark. Hands opened and closed themselves between faces that silently cried. Arms and legs kicked and grabbed helplessly, as if trying to find grip on something to pull themselves out of the tree. Ribcages sunk in and out, breathing. Hanging from the branches were cocooned human remains, swaying in the powerful mountaintop wind.

In front of the tree, a creature stood. Its fingers were roots, three of them on each hand. Mud bled over its eyes from a crown made of sticks, leaves and woodland trinkets. Its skin was a mixture of bark and white birch. A mouth breathed laboriously with stone teeth below its muddied eyes.

"What are you?" Ellie said.

The creature took two steps forward, pressed its long fingers against its filthy crown. Even without visible eyes, Ellie felt it looking at her. Something rose within her emotionally—like a great invisible hand sinking into her.

"I am the Donneur Vie," it said. Its mouth didn't move as it spoke, and its words chimed inside Ellie's head. Its voice was light and delicate, every word it enunciated slow and labored. It was like the voice of an ancient, withered woman speaking. "It was a mistake for you to come here."

"I came here because I had no other choice. Who are you—
what are you?"

The creature turned and looked up at the great big tree. The
bark, veins and muscles of the tree pulsated and heaved. "I have
existed for as long as this mountain has existed—this mountain
which has a snowy forehead." It looked back at Ellie. Its voice
was penetrating, almost vibrating in her mind. "I have been
given many names over the centuries—by the Abenaki, the
French, the English. I am the Great Soul of the mountain, and I
communicate with the spirits of the region."

"Of the forest, you mean. The Adrienne Forest?"

"That is the name the French gave it, yes."

"So you know all who have died in the forest?"

The creature nodded. "I hear all their voices. Once they're
here, they cannot leave. Their spirits are restless, wandering
those woods, crying out. They live in perpetual pain. I am here
to console those spirits, so that they are never alone."

Ellie felt her blood go cold, and she took two steps towards
the Donneur Vie. "If you can hear the spirits of all the forests'
dead, then you can tell me if Alan is still alive."

"Alan?"

"My son." The words came out hoarse. "Please tell me if
my son is still alive."

The creature looked up to the sky, and its lips peeled back. A grimace passed what little could be seen of its face. "Who is your son?"

"He's just a boy. Seventeen years old. He hasn't been well. He's come up here to do something that I'll never recover from."

"I understand the reputation of the forest. You really do believe that you can save him?"

"What else can I believe!" Ellie shouted, not realizing how desperate she sounded until it was out of her mouth. "I just want my son back. That's all I ask."

"Your journey to find your son is a path of truth."

"What are you talking about? Why did you bring me up here?"

"I can't give you the truth. The truth is your own journey—you must find it. But I can guide you towards it."

Ellie threw her hands up in frustration. "That's the exact same thing the Tinker told me. Both of you claim to want to 'guide' me to where my son is, all the while dancing around everything I need to know. Who should I believe at this point? I don't even understand what you are."

The Donneur Vie nodded, laced its shrubby hands together. "Your mistrust is understandable. But whether you choose to believe me or the Tinker is your greatest struggle, Ellie. You are just one of countless others who must make a decision like this."

"Enough with the vague talk. I'm not leaving without my son. I came here for a reason. Do you understand? That reason is somewhere in that forest down there"—she pointed off the pass—"and he's all I have left. I don't care who you are or what the Tinker wants. If you can't help me, then you've done nothing but waste my time. If you know where my son is, then tell me now."

It walked up to her, its long legs struggling against the wind, and held out a large mossy hand. Within its palm was a small silver key. It was old, slightly bent and rusty. Ellie considered the Donneur Vie's bioarboribus face, and despite its lack of any visible eyes, she felt its empathetic glare on her. She took the key and the creature stepped back.

"Your spirit is strong, Ellie," it said. "I can feel your determination. It is your strength, but also your weakness."

"Where do I need to use this key?"

The creature stretched one long fungi and moss strewn arm towards the forest. "Lake Franconia. Go there—that is where you'll find your son."

Ellie blinked, suddenly aghast with disbelief. This was it? After all that cryptic talk, this creature—this Soul of the Mountain—told her exactly where her son was? It seemed suspicious, but then again the Tinker wasn't exactly the most trustworthy person she'd encountered here either.

"That's where he is? Lake Franconia?"

"That is where you must go."

It wasn't answering her questions. It occurred to her then just how cold it was up here. Her face was stinging from the violent winds near the summit. If she stayed any longer, she may catch hypothermia.

"I'll leave you now, Ellie."

"Will I see you again?"

"I don't know. I can only wish you the best."

It began lumbering back towards the living tree. Each step it took was felt in the ground, even from where Ellie stood.

"Wait!" Ellie called.

The creature stopped, turned to look at her.

"Who is the Tinker? What is he?"

For a long time, the creature said nothing. Finally, it answered: "He is the reason why the forest knows so much death."

It went around the tree and vanished into the clouds. Ellie stood with the little key in her hand, staring at the living tree with macabre curiosity.

I'm closer to you now, she thought as she turned to leave the pass. *Please, don't give up on me now.*

Carefully, she descended the mountain.

Night was falling on the forest, and with every passing moment it grew colder. Ellie hurried down Summit Trail. Lack of sleep was wearing on her, and it felt like a strenuous endeavor to lift her feet off the ground with each step she took. Her eyelids sank and she had to force them open and shake her head as she went. It felt like she was spinning.

No longer could she keep her eyes open, and they shut. Accidentally she wandered a few paces off trail and tripped over a branch, then went head over feet down a steep hill.

"Shit!"

Down she went. She rolled, rocks and sticks jabbing into her ribs and legs. One of her arms snaked out to try and grab something but couldn't find any grip. It wasn't until she slammed against a tree at the bottom of the hill did she finally stop. She lay there, her world spinning.

"God damn it," she whispered, struggling to pull herself up. "God damn it all."

Everything hurt and her feet were struggling beneath her as if she were on an uneasy sea. Grabbing her aching ribs, she turned and found herself looking at a bloated face with a black tongue.

"Jesus fucking Christ!" Ellie staggered away and her back hit the tree she had just landed against. Her fingernails dug into its bark as she stared at the dead man in front of her.

The man hung from a low tree branch. It looked as if he had been hanging there for some time. His brown-green skin was hanging off his bones like sludge. Dark stains of wet decomposition seeped through his filthy flannel shirt and jeans. Maggots crawled in and out of his face and around his turgid tongue. The thick rope from which he hung sank so deep into his neck that it seemed as if he were hanging merely by his spine.

The stench was violating, burning Ellie's face. For several moments she was unable to piece together any cohesive thought. Then she looked down at the ground below the man's dangling boots. A collection of his personal belongings sat decaying in the grass and dirt; a leather wallet, a pair of scissors, a comb, an unused trash bag, and an old pair of glasses that had perhaps fallen off his face.

Carefully, Ellie crept towards the hanging body and snatched the wallet from beneath him. Within she found his driver's license. In the photo the man smiled, with a bright mop of curly red hair on his head and even some freckles across the bridge of his nose. Jacob Raymond Langley, thirty-seven years old, of Utica, New York. He left behind seventeen dollars. Between the bills, Ellie found a bent photograph of Jacob standing on a dock with a big blue lake behind him, a teenage boy in one arm, a blonde woman in the other, all smiling.

"I don't..." The wallet fell from her hands.

I don't know what to say to you, she thought, feeling foolish. *I don't know the circumstances that brought you here to this forest, but I'm so sorry that this is what's become of you. I see how you looked in that photograph, and I see who I think is your wife and child. I can only vaguely recognize you now—a few red hairs remain on your head, and I believe those are your glasses on the ground beneath your hanging feet. It seems like you've become a different entity now.*

Jacob Raymond Langley, is that who you still are? You don't look a thing like him anymore. Everything you were, everything your life was— your friends and family, your career, your passions and hobbies and memories. All of it is gone now. What made you feel that you deserved to die like this, Jacob? You didn't die of old age, surrounded by loved ones who wanted to fill your last moments with love. You died alone, miles from home, away from everyone who ever knew you. You died so alone that you have remained here in this forest, wasting away with no one to find you. I can't think of an unhappier way to die than how you did, Jacob. You couldn't have deserved this.

Ellie felt she could no longer stay with the dead man formally known as Jacob Langley. Wiping her face, she turned away and began to climb up the hill she had tumbled down, the pain throughout her body suddenly having gone numb. She left the corpse of Jacob Langley behind in its self-imposed tomb.

The dark had become so dense that Ellie had to use her flashlight. She hurried down Butte-de-Tahure, keeping an eye out for the yellow rope that would bring her back to the security of the old cabin. Memories of the night before haunted her. *The dead*, she kept thinking. *The forest's dead are out here.* Every tree that appeared in the beam of her light made her paranoid. Sometimes she mistook one for a soul.

She picked up the pace, trotting downhill. "Gotta get back," she whispered to herself, the freezing air blowing past her numb face. "Please be close, please be—"

She tripped and fell forward. Her hands shot ahead of her and she caught her fall, but the flashlight went airborne.

"No!" Ellie shouted.

It hit the ground and rolled away, going down a slope and out of sight. The beam of the flashlight shined against a cluster of trees ahead. It had ceased moving.

Ellie lay on the freezing ground, her knees and palms aching from the fall, her eyes firm on the light, convinced that the flashlight would begin rolling away again. When it didn't, she calmed down.

"Okay," she told herself. "Okay…"

It occurred to her now that she was in full darkness. The only source of light was the flashlight several feet ahead of her. The knowledge of this froze her in place, and she was suddenly afraid to move. Her mind began to play tricks on her. She looked behind her, convinced that something was there, but could see nothing. Carefully, she listened. There were no footsteps, no rustling of leaves or cracking twigs. Nothing.

Perhaps it was all some fear-induced placebo. She only felt like something was nearby because she was scared that there was. When she was a girl, she hated going to bed in the dark with her closet door open. As she lay in bed, she would stare at the closet, convinced that there was something in there watching her, even though she could see nothing at all. This paranoia wouldn't go away until she braved the dark, leapt across the room and slapped the light switch on. Only when she could see for herself that there was nothing in her closet except for coats and pants was she able to sleep.

Ellie took a deep breath. "Just coats and pants," she whispered to herself, now focused on the light ahead. "Pants and coats and shirts. That's all. Coats and pants… coats and pants…"

Slowly, she got to her feet, then scurried over to the ditch and snatched the flashlight up and spun it around herself, shining its light against the path behind her and at the trees to her sides. Her heart pounded in her ears, and she tried to listen. Complete silence.

After several paces down the trail, she stopped again. She noticed something, to her left off the path. Between the trees, she saw something was glowing.

Swallowing, Ellie went off the trail towards the light.

It looked like several candles, the glow of them capering against the darkness. They sat on a table covered with a dirty white cloth, in near tatters from exposure. Along with the candles were plates covered in grime and leaves.

What the hell is this? she thought.

She pointed the flashlight to her right and she found another dilapidated table. The ground was covered in old confetti and streamers. Between the tables was a steel easel with an artificial wreath on it. A ribbon hung from it, and "MATTHEW AND CASSANDRA SEPTEMBER 20TH, 2004" was inscribed on it.

Ellie pointed the flashlight to her left. Just at the edge of the light, she saw a small mahogany stage with a white wooden fence lining the back of it. In its center was a crumbling ceremonial arch. Sticks and pine needles covered the stage, and the arch stood crooked from a branch that had fallen on top of it.

Swallowing, Ellie approached the stage, then stopped. She felt as if something was watching her. The hairs on her arms went erect. She pointed the flashlight all around herself, seeing only the old tables around her.

Out there, somewhere in that forest, she heard crying. Those cries then became shrill howls of agony, going low into exhausted sobs, then rising into anguished wails.

Ellie turned and bolted away from the remains of the old wedding.

The trail, where is the fucking trail?

In the darkness, she had difficulty figuring out where she had come from. Those screams followed her in the dark, getting louder. They propelled her forward.

"Fuck get me out of here."

Just then she went over a narrow crevasse and her feet landed in water up to her shins. The shock of the freezing water made her squeal and she grabbed at a rock in front of her to keep from falling over. She pointed the light around herself, realizing that she had fallen into a ravine.

The ravine was shallow and she could climb out—dry land was at eye level. She grabbed the ledge and began pulling herself up, but there was something weighing on her leg. She pointed the flashlight at the water below and saw a gray arm latched onto her ankle.

That was when the terror, which had been building up inside her since it grew dark, finally unleashed itself. Ellie screamed at the top of her lungs, lost her grip on the ledge and fell back into the freezing water.

A bog corpse rose from the waters, its empty sockets staring at her. Its leathery mouth moved, trying to speak to her.

"Please help me," it said.

Adrenaline fueling her, Ellie tore her leg from the corpse's grip, flung herself around and got back on her feet. She retreated up the ravine, the icy water splashing with each stomp. Eventually the ravine went upwards, and she climbed out and found herself back on the trail.

All around her, Ellie heard voices whispering from the trees. She hauled herself down the trail, trying her best to keep her flashlight steady ahead of her.

The tree with the yellow rope appeared like a north star. Ellie ran to it, stopped, and rested her hand on it. An awful compulsion came over her, and she turned and shined her light down the path. A dead person floated towards her with its feet dangling two feet above the ground, creeping into the beam of her light.

"Leave me alone!" she screamed.

She ran off the trail, following the yellow rope, not daring to stop again. The rotting old cabin appeared in her light. She leapt inside, slammed the door shut and pulled the dresser in front of it. After shutting her flashlight off she planted herself in the corner again and began to cry.

"Why?" she asked. "What do you want from me? I just want my son back."

For a long time, she prayed for daylight to come and rescue her. From her backpack she took the heavy wool blanket and wrapped it around herself tightly. Her teeth chattered and her whole body trembled from terror and cold. The blanket warmed her, but it did little to ease her trauma. She wanted to be out of this horrible forest. She hoped that Alan would still be here, by the end of this mess.

By some miracle she had fallen asleep. Her emotional and physical exhaustion became so extreme that she managed to pass out despite her duress, and she slept for the remainder of the night.

Daylight remained gray and spectral when she woke up. The events of the previous day remained with her strongly. That bedroom light had been flipped on and the coats and pants in the dark closet had taken their natural form. The dead were gone. For now.

It occurred to her that she was still slightly wet from falling into the ravine, but her pants had mostly dried. She kept the wool blanket wrapped firmly around herself, rubbing her arms.

A sneeze left her face. *God,* she thought, *of all my problems, the last thing I need is pneumonia.*

The faint sound of raindrops danced on the roof. Outside, the world was glazed over with rainwater. When she slipped her hands into her pockets, she felt the key from the Donneur Vie and remembered where she needed to go next. She took out her map and scanned it over until she found Lake Franconia. In order to get there, she needed to take Désespoir Trail. She got up, moved the dresser and stepped outside.

On the rock where she had sat during her campfire was a wet folded up piece of paper held in place by a stone. Ellie removed the stone, carefully picked up the paper and peeled it open. It was a note, the ink inside bleeding from the rain:

I know you've been in cahoots with that thing living on the summit of the mountain. Don't listen to a goddamn word it gives you. You came here for a very important reason... and I can be the one to give it to you. That thing can't give you what you really need. It can only give you the status quo. It WANTS to lead you astray, Ellie. But me? I can give you change. But we'll see where you are when you finally do find Alan at the end of all this.

Adieu, Mademoiselle Jackson. Or is it Rodriguez?

It was left unsigned. There were many things to puzzle over regarding this cryptic message from the Tinker, but why in particular did he feel the need to address her by her maiden name?

Clancy came to mind. She dropped the note and dug out her phone and stared at the black screen. It had been off since her pit stop at the observation platform. That was now two days ago. There must have been dozens of messages from her husband by now, but they were messages she couldn't afford to see or hear. He would just be trying to persuade her.

I'm sorry, Clancy, she thought, returning the phone to her pocket, *but I'm closer now than ever before. I promise you, things will be better. Soon.*

The hike took roughly two hours, from one end of the forest to the other. Eventually she found herself standing before Lake Franconia, an expansive body of water. According to her map, from where she stood in Clarke's Purchase, she would have been able to see Jefferson across the lake. Yet, the perpetual fog that submerged this forest didn't allow it. It lingered over the dark waters like a curtain.

This was where she needed to be. Yet, what was she supposed to be looking for?

For a long time she walked along the shore of the lake, watching water ripples crawl up the mud and then pull back into the quagmire. How many people had drowned themselves in these waters? How many parents took their children out fishing on this lake, unaware of the tragedies lying on the bottom?

She didn't want to think about any of this. She couldn't. Instead, her mind wandered to more pleasant thoughts— specifically the memories of her pregnancy with Alan.

It felt like centuries ago. Truth be told, neither Clancy nor Ellie wanted to have kids. After they got married at an Oriental garden in Providence, they moved to a small apartment in Quincy, south of Boston.

It was a cramped little place, but it was somewhere that Ellie looked back on with a tug of affection. It had a little upstairs bedroom with a small window, and the living room, kitchen and bathroom were all downstairs. The sound of MBTA trains going back and forth was constant, rushing by the apartment and rattling the silverware in the cupboards. Sometimes it woke them up in the middle of the night, and at the time it pissed them both off, but now as Ellie thought back to it, she couldn't help but smile.

Clancy began his graduate degree part time at Boston University, hoping to iron out his business aspirations. When he wasn't doing that, he was working as a security guard on campus.

Ellie waited tables at a diner and even did some taxicab work. Both were busy, and there were some days where they didn't see each other at all. When they did find themselves in the same room, they embraced the time they had together.

It wasn't easy, starting a new life with somebody. Ellie supposed it never really is. When Ellie was a week late on her period and suddenly started vomiting at work, alarm bells went off. A pregnancy test confirmed her suspicions. Even while being safe—somehow, it had happened.

That had been the most terrifying day of Eleanor's life. She sat on the living room couch, staring blankly at the TV as it played some soap opera without paying attention to it. Every few minutes she eyed the clock, knowing Clancy was coming home from class soon. When the front door opened and she heard his footsteps, she closed her eyes and just wanted to cry.

"Hey Ellie," he said with a bright, surprised grin. "You're home early."

"Yeah."

Clancy went into the kitchen and began sifting through the refrigerator. "You know, this semester can't be over soon enough."

Ellie got up slowly, and like a ghost she wandered to the kitchen, standing in the doorway with her arms crossed over her belly.

"That teacher has got a stick up her ass or something—I swear she's got it out for me. I don't know what I'm doing wrong with the assignment, but her vague instructions aren't exactly ideal," he went on.

There was no easy way to approach this. For a long time she just stood there, shifting from one foot to the other, trying to think up a good way to say what she needed to say.

She just said it: "I'm pregnant."

A rack in the fridge and everything on it clattered as Clancy accidentally hit his head against it. A few soda cans fell out and rolled onto the floor. He managed to pull his head out and stand up straight. "What?"

"I'm pregnant," she said again.

For a moment he laughed, then looked at her seriously. "What? You're sure?"

"I left work early today and had a test."

Silence came between them, and perhaps it wasn't very long, but it felt like a lifetime. Slowly, she felt tears push out from behind her eyes.

"I don't know what to do," she said.

"I don't"—Clancy stammered—"how—why?"

All at once emotion came over her, and she found herself pressing her hands against her face and leaving the kitchen, going for the front door.

"Ellie, wait!"

She was already at the door, stepping out. She had to get out of there. All of this was far too much for her at once. She needed to be alone.

That evening, she took the Red Line to Wollaston Beach. Upon emerging from the subway, she crossed the street and stood at the waist high concrete barrier separating the city from the beach. The sun wasn't all the way down yet, but its bottom was touching the water at the edge of the world, and the sky began to turn a quiet velvet. She climbed over the barrier and walked towards the water.

When she reached the point where the sand was wet and gray, she sat down. She watched the sun go down. Her mind was abuzz with all sorts of conflicting ideas.

A mother? How could she be? She saw the struggles her own mother faced growing up in Lawrence, managing that little overcrowded duplex. It seemed like her mother had lost twenty years of her life. She remembered the hysterical crying, the stress-induced manic fits, and the terror that seemed to seize her mother over any little cough.

Abortion. That was what her mind kept telling her. She couldn't have a baby—how could she? Her husband was still in school, and she wasn't swimming in money at her waitress gig. Yet, just thinking of that word—*abortion*—filled her with malady.

It terrified her, the idea of being a mother, but it also terrified her to not have the baby at all.

When the sun finally vanished, taking the natural light of the world with it, Ellie stood and returned to the subway, taking the Red Line back to Quincy Adams station. From there, she walked fifteen minutes back to the apartment.

Dread filled her as she unlocked the front door. She was terrified that Clancy wouldn't be there—that he had packed his bags and left. When she stepped inside, something else awaited her.

All the lights were off. A dim glow came from the kitchen. On the table, a little chocolate cheesecake from the bakery down the street was set. A little candle was erected in the middle of it.

Clancy emerged from the shadows. The look on his face was apprehensive. "Ellie."

The whole setup brought the tears back again—tears of both happiness and relief. She hugged him tightly.

"I don't know what to do, Clancy," she told him. "I'm scared."

"I'm scared too."

"I don't know whether to keep it or not."

"I don't either."

"Should we just wait?"

He kissed her temple. "If you want to wait a little bit, we can. We don't have to make any decisions now."

That seemed like the most comfortable decision they could make. This decision wound up being the right one. As time went on, and Ellie's belly began to grow, both became cheerier. They walked and talked with an excited air, eager for the future. It was unspoken between them, but they had both decided to have the child. Three months after that day, they began shopping for a crib.

On August 29th, Ellie's water broke at six o' clock in the morning. It woke her and Clancy out of exhausted sleep, and both were immediately aware of just how moist the bed had become. They rushed to Quincy Medical. Clancy was there the entire time, holding Ellie's hand, whispering into her ear as she pushed and pushed. When the baby came, the doctor made a quick, rudimentary inspection of the child. The boy already had little black hairs on his scalp, and he made a couple of quiet yelps, but was otherwise quiet.

"I present Alan Richard, Mrs. Jackson," the doctor said, placing the baby gently into the new mother's arms.

The child's dark brown eyes looked up at her, knowing instinctively that this was his mother. He pressed his face against her breast and made another little yelp. Ellie's hands were trembling from the shock and rush of it all, and she had to focus to keep her composure. If it were possible, she wanted to live in that moment for all eternity. That day had been the happiest of her entire life.

Caught up in this daydream, Ellie tripped over a large branch and toppled onto her hands and knees. "Fucking shit!" she shouted. Her hands had managed to catch the fall, and they got all scraped up. Grumbling, she got back up and wiped her palms against her pants.

She decided to take a short break and sat down in the grass, picking at some rocks in the dirt between her feet. She kept thinking of Alan's birth. She wished she could experience it all again. Clancy sobbed the moment he saw the child—tears literally pouring down his face—and thinking of this made her chuckle. There wasn't another man on this planet she would have rather had a child with.

Once satisfied with her memories, Ellie stood back up and continued walking around the lake, keeping her eyes peeled.

A small cavern appeared in the ground ahead, about two meters away from shore. Ellie approached it. A cold breeze crept out, and she could barely see anything inside. She took out her flashlight and shined it in. It went deep enough to where no natural light could touch the bottom.

Ellie descended into it.

Darkness ingested her. The rock walls and ceiling dripped with water and her boots sank into the soft wet ground. Sitting in the mud ahead of her was an old suitcase. It was strewn with moss and the leather was withered and torn. Beneath the handle was a lock with a keyhole. On top of the suitcase was what looked like a manila folder inside a plastic bag.

Raising an eyebrow, Ellie knelt before the suitcase. She picked up the manila folder and removed it from the plastic bag. After wiping away some of the dirt, she saw "RODRIGUEZ, ELEANOR CARLA #444" scribbled on the front in black marker.

What the hell is this?

She opened the folder and saw dozens of yellowing documents stuffed inside. She set it on the ground next to her and turned her attention to the suitcase instead.

From her coat she took out the key the Donneur Vie had given her. This was what it wanted her to find. Nerves set a fire inside her ribcage. Beads of sweat rolled down her temples as she lifted the handle of the suitcase and carefully slipped the key into the lock and turned it. *Click.* The lock clips flipped up. What Ellie found within made her gasp, stand and leap away.

Bones were stuffed messily in the suitcase. Small bones—a child's bones. A skull peeked out sadly at her from within.

Ellie's hands pressed over her mouth and her eyes filled with tears. "No. No... why?"

For a long time, she could do nothing but stare at those bones, her mind filling with all sorts of conflicting and heinous thoughts. Scorching agony filled her veins. She wanted to vomit. She wanted to tear her teeth out. She couldn't stop looking, but at the same time if she kept looking then she would shatter into a thousand pieces. She turned away, digging her fingers into her eyes, sobbing.

"Alan," she whispered, "I want you back. I wanted you back... please come back to me."

Come Forth in Thaw

II.

Psalm for the Storm

Come Forth in Thaw

MCLEAN HOSPITAL – BELMONT, MA

DATE: NOV. 15, 2017

SUB: RODRIGUEZ, ELEANOR CARLA

REFERRED: JACKSON, CLANCY (former spouse)

ASSIGN: DR. JAMES BALDRICK

NOTE: Ellie's back, once again admitted by her ex-hubby. I probably should have expected it by now, given the anniversary of what happened was last month. She's not thrilled to be here again. I've had her dosages upped and I've been speaking with her every other day. I wanted to be sure before she was turned over to you, but it's become clear to me that once again she's beginning to "relapse." Miserable.

Baldrick, in case you don't already know, I'll fill you in. Ms. Rodriguez had a son with her now former husband Clancy named Alan. About eight years ago, on October 13th 2009, when Ellie was twenty-nine, her son went missing. A year later, the child's body was found in a suitcase in Connecticut, and her marriage crumbled not long after. I'll fill you in on the details another time in person but for now, I'd like you to have a head start on what you're about to deal with.

Be prepared, Baldrick. Ellie is an exhausting patient, and this isn't her first, second, or even third rodeo here at McLean. There are two parts of Ellie that are at odds with one another. One of them is grounded in reality. The other is pure delusion.

When Ellie is "in" reality, she had no sense of self-preservation. She's attempted suicide at least three times during her previous visits here. Once she tried hanging herself by her socks. Another time she smashed a window and began grinding her wrists against the shattered glass in the frame. The last time, perhaps around 2015, she clogged the drain of a bathroom sink and tried to drown herself. She's been under suicide watch numerous times and the only time she seems "stable" is when she's medicated—with hard stuff.

Suicide ideation is a significant part of her prognosis. The last time she was here in September of 2016, she kept an old notebook with her, and kept drawing pictures and writing about this forest up north in the White Mountains—that Adrienne Forest or whatever it's called. To my understanding it's one of those suicide "hot spots" like the Golden Gate

Bridge. Her fixation and fantasy of it is unhealthy. She romanticizes it in her writing. On the final page of her journal she taped a newspaper clipping about a body being found there, along with a drawing she had done. The drawing is a shadow of someone standing within the forest—I'm assuming it's her. Bodies hang from the branches all around her, and the roots of the trees seem to turn into hands beneath her, reaching up to pull her into the ground.

Secondly, Ellie has what I refer to as "relapses." These are her delusions. She slides psychologically out of reality. Occasionally, she "slips" back to that day—October 13th 2009, the day her son Alan vanished. She becomes convinced that she can still "rescue" him somehow, as if his body was never discovered and he's still out there. Her denial of her son's death is devastating to her mental development, because when reality does come crashing down on her again, the suicidal tendencies become pronounced and unpredictable. KEEP A CLOSE EYE ON HER, BALDRICK.

Despite their marriage dissolving, her ex-husband seems to love her still, and he comes in often to visit her. When he's here Ellie seems somewhat okay. In between treatments, always allow Clancy in.

If you have any questions or need help, tell me. I'm sure your first meeting with her will be worth talking about. I'll also give you a list of the medications I've prescribed her.

Best of luck,

Daniel Howell, PhD

DR. F. REILEY BALDRICK

Date: 1/20/18

Sub: E.C. RODRIGUEZ

After two months of close work, I've decided that Ms. Rodriguez has no further benefit staying at McLean for the time being. I've upped her medications and she's hasn't had any serious fits over the past four odd weeks. I've spoken with her ex-husband (C. Jackson) and I've decided that she should have some time outside of the hospital. I've suggested that Mr. Jackson take her somewhere quiet, away from Boston, preferably in nature. I've also instructed him to contact me directly if any digressions in Ms. Rodriguez's behavior is noted. She'll be out by the end of the month, tops.

Baldrick

It was all gone. The rusty autumn leaves vanished, and a thick blanket of February snow blanketed the world around her. This was the world Ellie had always been in. That October day was long gone. There was no hope. No Alan. No purpose.

Since slipping out of her relapsed delusion, Ellie stayed at the ruined cabin, staring at herself in a murky mirror, sobbing. Her dark hair had noticeable grey streaks, and aged lines were carved into her withered face. Her eyes were cloudy and looked like shining pebbles glittering out of two dark ponds. No, this wasn't the twenty-nine-year-old woman from all those years ago. She was a thirty-eight-year-old grieving mother who had lost all reason to go on living.

She read over the medical paperwork from her doctors that she had found with the suitcase. She already understood everything even before she finished them. The reality of her world was crushing, and she knew that this wasn't the first time she was experiencing it. When her mind slipped away into believing that Alan could still be saved, she savored the comfort and purpose that fantasy gave her. Yet when the fabrics of that fantasy began to pull away, like the single thread of a blanket being pulled to untangle the whole thing, the reality was so soul-crushing that she couldn't bear to live it.

"Alan" she whispered, looking at her pathetic reflection in the filthy mirror. She held her locket tight in her fist. "I'm sorry. I'm so sorry."

Nine long years had passed since that afternoon when she had taken her son to the Assembly Row Marketplace on that October day. Clancy was in Cambridge at the time and he asked Ellie to pick up a carry-on bag for him so he could take it on a business flight with him to Phoenix. Alan, her eight-year-old baby boy, her world, with the brown eyes and dark skin of his mother and the curly hair and square jaw of his father, went with her. Ellie decided that while she was there, she would get new shoes for him.

Alan had been exhausting that day, running ahead of Ellie despite her protests, going from one shop window to another, saying this and that. Eventually she got the boy to settle and even had him by the hand. After getting Clancy's carry-on bag, she took Alan into a shoe store. At the back were rows of boxes filled with shoes, and Ellie told Alan to sit on a chair behind her while she browsed.

Obediently, Alan sat on the chair, no more than two feet away. After looking through two boxes, Ellie looked back at him. It was the last time she would ever see him. There he sat, smiling brightly and patiently, his hands on his knees, kicking his feet under the space beneath his chair. Ellie grinned at him and looked away, and while she didn't realize it in that moment, he was gone forever from then on.

Another two boxes were browsed, and Ellie found a pair befitting her child. "Hey Alan," she said, holding the sneakers up and turning around, "these look a bit like—"

There was nothing but an empty chair behind her. Puzzled and irritated, Ellie groaned: "Alan! Get back here!"

After putting the shoes away, she went around the store calling his name, becoming less irritated and more alarmed. Eventually she spoke with management, asking if they had seen a mixed race eight-year-old boy with curly hair and dark skin wandering around alone. The woman running the store said she hadn't, then contacted mall security.

Ellie sat anxiously outside the security room, twiddling her fingers, hoping that her son had just wandered away and gotten lost. This hope was shattered when she saw the face of the security guard stepping out to speak with her.

"We've contacted the Somerville police," he told her.

Ellie's heart leapt into her throat and she stood. "What?"

"Come in for a moment."

The guard took her into the room and stood her before a large monitor. On the screen, she could see a man wearing a gray hoodie and faded jeans leading her son out of the back entrance of the mall among a crowd.

"Do you recognize this man?" the guard asked, pointing.

"No, I don't. Who is he? Do you know where my son is?"

"Somerville P.D. are on their way. They're going to section off an area around the mall, begin a search, and ask you a few questions. An Amber Alert has been put out."

The floor felt like quicksand. All the worst scenarios played out in her head and one trembling hand came up against her feverish forehead. Before she fell apart, she careened out of the security room and dialed Clancy, telling him to come to Assembly Row immediately.

The following thirteen months became an obsession. For three hundred and eighty five days, Ellie's thoughts were fixated on the single image she had seen on that monitor, of that man in the gray hoodie, walking with her child. His hand had been on Alan's back as if he were some sort of protective father figure. The lack of closure was destroying Ellie. During the final months, she was unable to work or even get out of bed. Her mind couldn't be controlled. All she could think about was Alan.

All of it came to a bleak, miserable end in November the following year. Two boys, both eleven, were walking home from school one afternoon in Branford, Connecticut. They decided to take a shortcut home and cut through some woods, following a rusty pair of railroad tracks. They came upon an old leather suitcase that had no earthly reason for being there, sitting within some tall grass next to the tracks. The boys opened the briefcase, and what they found inside sent them fleeing home as fast as they could, pleading to their parents to call the police.

A light went out inside Ellie as a Connecticut State Trooper broke the news to her over the phone. She stood with the receiver against her ear, numb from the words going through the line.

"Are you there, Mrs. Jackson?" the trooper asked.

"I'm here."

The trooper informed her that two Massachusetts staties would be arriving her house later that evening. Ellie thanked the trooper and hung up. For the rest of the day Ellie did menial tasks around the house like a ghost, as if she had just walked away from a traumatic car accident. She did the laundry, vacuumed, stocked the refrigerator. Every movement she made was animated and lifeless. Her mind and soul were far away.

When Clancy came home, Ellie told him the news. "They found Alan," she said with no expression.

Clancy's eyes filled with tears, and he dropped the groceries that he had brought in and seized his wife by the wrists. "Where is he?"

"In a suitcase," Ellie replied. "He's nothing but bones now, I guess."

The color drained from Clancy's face. He let go of Ellie, suddenly lightheaded, and leaned against a wall to catch his fall.

"I'm going outside to weed the garden now," Ellie said.

Clancy glared at her, offended. Yet, he realized that there was something deeply wrong with his wife. Ellie wasn't blinking, and her face was still and sickly. Every word she spoke sounded like an automated messaging machine rather than a human being. When she turned to leave, her body was stiff and jerky.

This state of disassociation continued for the next few days. She spoke with a few Somerville police officers and state troopers, answering their questions patiently, clearly, and lifelessly without any outward show of emotion. She continued her chores, watched television, and ignored Clancy's pleas for her to speak to him about how she was feeling.

The breaking point came a week after the discovery. Ellie was in the kitchen scrubbing dishes with a sponge. She was working at a plate that had some hardened cheese stuck to it, and no matter how much she scrubbed, it wouldn't come off.

Flustered, Ellie applied more soap and began using a rougher sponge. The cheese didn't budge.

"Come on," Ellie said, her voice cracking. She scrubbed harder, but it still wasn't coming off. "I said come on!"

She scrubbed so hard that the plate began to slip from her grip. Tears rolled down her cheeks.

"Come on. Come on! Come on, come on, COME ON, COME ON, COME ON!"

The cheese wouldn't come off.

"YOU FUCKING PIECE OF SHIT!"

Ellie threw the plate across the kitchen. It shattered against a wall and fell to the floor in pieces. Ellie scowled at its remains, her lungs heaving and her hands shaking. She went around the kitchen yanking open cupboards and tearing out plates and silverware and smashing them against the floor.

"You son of a bitch!" she kept shouting. "Son of a bitch! How could you? How fucking could you?"

Then she went into the living room, where she flipped over the couch, stomped her foot through the coffee table and kicked over the television, which fell to the ground in violent sparks. She grabbed the ceiling fan, and with insane rage tore it out of the ceiling and threw it through a window.

Next she charged into her bedroom and tore the sheets off her bed and smashed the mirror over the nightstand. She chucked her vanity to the floor, and its contents of makeup and hairbrushes and jewelry spilled everywhere. Ellie rampaged through her home, screaming and crying, destroying everything that got in her way.

Then came Alan's room. She shoved the door open and stepped in. It hadn't been touched since the day he went missing the previous October. His bed was still unmade, all his clothes were still folded up in his dresser. His stuffed animal Mr. Wolf was sitting on the carpet near a dozen green army men frozen in mid-battle.

"Alan," Ellie croaked.

The rage drained, and all that remained was the sad and hollow shell of a grieving mother who was no longer a mother. Ellie wobbled across the room and fell to the floor and took Mr. Wolf in her arms, clutching it against her chest, covering it in kisses.

"Alan," she grieved, "come back to me. Please come back to me. I miss you so much. I want you back. God can have his own goddamned child, but not you. You'll always be mine." A groan left her as she cuddled her dead son's stuffed animal. "I'm so lonely here. Can you forgive me? Please... can you forgive me?"

The dark shape of the worn out thirty-eight-year-old Eleanor Rodriguez stood like a grotesque hunchback in the mirror. All the repressed memories came seeping back. And with those memories came that instinctive compulsion.

The noose hung from the rafters, seeming to coquet her with seductive implications. She had come here and tied the yellow rope around the trees leading to this abandoned cabin herself. It was her that had tied that noose and hung it from the rafters. It was her who nailed Mr. Wolf to a tree out of contempt for a world that had denied her child.

The Tinker's voice whispered to her: "What is hidden in snow will come forth in thaw."

The front door was open and she could see outside. It was the late evening—almost night. White flakes fluttered down through the dead branches above to the snow-covered ground. The shape of the Tinker could be seen out there, standing next to his wagon in the dark, an orange glow against his face from the cigarette burning in his mouth.

Ellie stepped outside. "What do you want from me?"

The Tinker cleared his throat. "My condolences, mademoiselle. You knew it was going to come to this. I told you not to go see that son of a bitch at the top of the mountain. Look at what he's done—you were much happier when it was just you and me."

"Leave me alone, Tinker."

"I'm not leaving until you give me what I want." The Tinker snapped his cigarette away.

"What do you want?"

"You know what that is." He held a rough hand out to her.

Ellie gripped her locket. "No. Never."

The Tinker shook his head at her. "You got no business with that locket anymore. You know that."

"I won't let you have it."

"I'll take good care of it. You've seen my other trinkets—all clean and cared for. Yours will see the same love and attention." The Tinker stepped forward, his eyes mad with hunger. "He was your responsibility, you know. As a mother, you failed. He'd still be alive if you just kept your eye on him."

Ellie pressed her hands against her ears. "Please…"

The Tinker took another step forward. "You don't deserve that locket and you know it. You're a fucking worthless excuse for a mother, allowing your own eight-year-old boy to die. Left him to die and get cut up and ditched inside of a suitcase like trash."

"Stop it!"

"No way." Another step forward. "You know I'm right. You're a failure. You think Clancy divorced you just because things got tough after you killed your kid? Nah. You're a burden. Imagine how much happier he would be if you just died. He could move on with his life, not carting his fucked-up ex-wife around from hospital to hospital, managing her medications, dealing with her violence, sending him on wild goose chases—"

"No!"

"Yes! The world would be better off without a crazy old lady who has nothing to be proud of. Career? Gone. Motherhood? Gone. Loving life partner? Don't even joke. When you die Clancy will be kicking his heels! 'Thank the stars!' he'll say, 'My worthless ex-wife is finally off my back! Now I can remarry and have another kid, and this time the mother will actually give a shit!' How exactly do you contribute to society? Wasting precious taxpayer money while you grub off the state for your medicine and hospital visits."

"Please…"

"Just give me your fucking locket already and be done with it, Eleanor. The sooner, the better."

Unable to take it anymore, Ellie fled into the cabin. She shut the door and pulled the dresser in front of it. The Tinker's footsteps crunched through the snow up to the front steps. "I can wait here for all eternity, Eleanor. Can you?"

Everything the Tinker told her sank deep into her soul. Ellie's eyes settled on the noose. She took a step towards it. Then she recoiled away. "No," she told herself. Images of the dead girl in the tent and the decomposing body of Jacob Langley came to her, powerful enough to repel her from the noose.

"What exactly is so appalling about it, Eleanor?" the Tinker whispered through the door. "Isn't that what you deserve? To die here, alone? To be unfound, forgotten and ungrieved?

Rotting? You don't deserve an honorable or natural death, Ellie. Not for somebody as pathetic as you. No… you deserve this. You know you do."

The noose seemed alluring again. Ellie considered it, listening to the Tinker, but terror kept her in place. "I can't," she choked. "I'm scared. I don't want to do it, but I need to."

"Wanna know the interesting thing about trauma?" the Tinker said. "It doesn't hit you right away. You know when you get punched in the face? The pain doesn't come immediately. A tingly numbness gets you first, and you sink into all this cloudiness for a while. Then, slowly, it all starts creeping in like a sinking ship. There comes a point when something can affect you so profoundly that it takes everything from you. Your thoughts, your beliefs, your whole damn identity. After that, there's nothing left but this empty space where a soul should have been. All of it robbed from you. Just one thing left in that void—the desire to die."

Ellie closed her eyes and swallowed. The Tinker's words felt natural and right. When she opened her eyes again, the noose waited for her. Ellie allowed her hand to reach up and caress it with her fingers.

"Camus once proposed that there is only one truly philosophical question, and that is deciding whether life is or is not worth living. That decision is yours. You have that power over life and death. The world can take everything from you, but it cannot deny you that."

There was just one thing left to do. Ellie took out her phone. If she was going to do this—leave this world—then she felt that she owed Clancy an apology. She wanted to tell him that she was sorry for failing to protect his son, and that soon she would avenge his death. She would no longer burden him, and he would finally be free. She wanted to wish him a happy life and a final farewell.

Ellie knelt on the cold dirty floor and turned her phone on for the first time in days. The screen lit up, bringing light into the dark cabin, and she was met with her home screen. A voice message greeted her, sent just an hour ago. Unable to help herself, Ellie played it and held the phone to her ear.

"Ellie," Clancy began, "I'm sorry. I know your phone is off, but I hope you will hear this. I'm sorry for everything. I know that you're in this forest. I don't know if you've gone and done it yet, but I pray that you haven't. If leaving you this message does anything… I hope to God I'm not too late getting here. This is my last hope."

The grief, which had strangled Ellie's heart to near death, had loosened its grip. *Clancy is here?* she thought. *He's in the forest?*

"I love you, Ellie. I know we're separated, but you are such a huge part of my world. I have the honor of having you. We've known each other for more than half our lives. I love you and I'll never stop loving you because you've created something with me. What we brought into this world together may not be here anymore, but that's why it's important that you stay alive.

"It's not your fault, Ellie. You were everything anyone could have wanted in a mother and wife. You were the mother of my child. For that gift, as short lived as it may have been, is something I will always be indebted to you for. And that's why you need to live, Ellie." Clancy's voice broke. "It's our duty as Alan's parents to keep who he was alive. Every memory we have of him—his birthdays, his first words, his first steps—if you go, Ellie, all those moments of him, the last things we have of him, will be lost. You need to live for me, baby. If you die, then I'm not only losing you, but what is left of Alan. Memory is a form of existence, isn't it?"

A long pause came over the message. Now she could hear Clancy crying. "Please come back, Ellie. I can't lose you too. I don't think I can survive it. If you can hear this, if it's not too late… come back. Please. Live, for Alan if not for anyone else."

The message ended. Ellie knelt there with the phone against her ear, letting Clancy's message sink in. Slowly, she got to her feet and put her phone away. The noose hung before her. It filled her with vile nausea.

"I'm sorry, Alan," she said.

She drew her knife from her pocket, snapped it open, cut the noose down and threw it across the room.

"What are you doing?" The Tinker barked, banging on the door. "You can't do this!"

Ellie wielded the knife before her. The Tinker slammed into the door, and the dresser in front of it rattled and tilted.

"I don't need you, Tinker," she said.

"Bullshit you don't. Open this damn door now. Don't make me come in there."

Another shove against the door came, and the dresser toppled over. The Tinker banged the door against the dresser until it moved out of the way. He stood in the doorway with a ferocious, offended glare.

"Ellie," he said slowly. "Remember everything I told you."

"I already knew everything you told me. I don't need it."

"Come to me."

"No."

"I said *COME TO ME!*"

The Tinker leapt forward like a leopard, and Ellie shuffled to one side. He narrowly missed her and landed against the small refrigerator. Seizing the opportunity, Ellie jabbed the knife into the middle of his back and fled. The Tinker shrieked, grabbed at the middle of his back, but was unable to reach the protruding handle of the knife.

"You piece of shit!" he roared.

The open doorway called her. She fled out of the cabin, her boots sinking into the ankle-high snow, and made a break into the trees.

The Tinker's voice followed her through the woods: "You can't escape from me, Ellie—do you know what I am? You belong to me!"

It was now full dark. Having forgotten the flashlight in the cabin, Ellie ran through pitch-blackness. Her hands flailed in front of herself, slapping away branches and feeling for any obstacles. Where was the trail? Where was anything. All she knew was that she had to get away from the Tinker as fast as she could.

Somewhere far off ahead she saw a light. A pale white light, shimmering in this black abyss. She went for it, not knowing any other direction to go. As she neared it, the trees spread out, and she found herself arriving at a steep cliff.

It was the bright moonlight in the clear winter sky that had guided her here, and that moonlight illuminated a wooden platform with a steel railing for a gondola lift. The green and red cable car swung in the freezing mountain breeze, creaking on its cables. Its windows were covered in frost, and its folding door was lined with rust. It looked to have been in disuse for a long time. Ellie stepped up to the railing of the platform and looked over.

This was probably only a quarter of the way up the mountain, but the drop was long enough to kill. Rock and granite covered the ground below—if she were to fall, it would be an ugly death. The story of the forlorn bride who jumped to her death entered Ellie's mind, and her guts churned at the memories of the screaming she had heard the night before.

"Ellie, Ellie, Ellie!" the Tinker's voice called from behind her. "You're running around in circles, Ellie! How many times do we have to do this god damned waltz? You'll just come back to me! If not now, then again soon!"

It was a dead end. The only thing she could do was hide. She went to the doors of the cable car and slithered her fingers into the jamb, then tried to pull it open. The rusty doors creaked and the ice in its hinges cracked. It wouldn't budge.

"Come on, come on!" Ellie grunted

She managed to force the doors open a few inches. She could see the inside—tattered leather seats with foam spilling out, and an old control panel with broken dials and levers. It was out of operation, but maybe she could hide. If she could just slip—

"Ellie!"

Her body froze. Slowly, she turned and saw the Tinker standing about ten feet behind her. He spun the blade she had stuck into him against his palm. Black blood smeared its steel.

He clicked his tongue. "Girl, you got some fight in you, I'll give you that." He chucked the knife to the ground. It landed point first into the soil, and its handle stuck upwards like a little Excalibur.

"Leave me alone," Ellie said, backing up against the door of the cable car. Unexpectedly it shifted away from the platform by her weight and the breeze. Ellie gasped and latched onto the railing. Between the edge of the platform and the cable car she could see those rocks below threatening her.

"You know why I can't leave you, Ellie. That's why you've got to stop fighting. It's best to just end it all right now. It's a Sisyphean task, going on like this."

"I said no!" Ellie regained her balance on the platform and faced the Tinker. She didn't want to look away from him. Her heart jackhammered in her chest, but she did not avert her gaze.

The Tinker grinned. His cap and hoodie shadowed his face, and that smile became pronounced against his hidden features. "Suicide, in its most sincere form, is a seed that takes hold in the heart. It's nurtured affectionately by listlessness and hopelessness. That seed grows, branching out from the heart, entering your veins, poisoning your blood. It enters every part of your body until you are consumed."

"I don't want to die."

"Yes you do." He lifted his hand up and twiddled his fingers at her. "Do you remember what I said about no touchies, Ellie? You'll give your locket to me. You'll give yourself to me. They *always* do. Every last one."

Ellie gritted her teeth. Instinct told her to press herself against the cable car again, but she had to keep herself from doing it. The danger of falling was too great. All she could do was stand there, her hands closing into fists and opening, watching as the Tinker approached with his touch of influence.

"I don't need any knife to get the job done," he said. His boots clunked against the wooden planks of the platform. Now he was merely five feet away. "The best weapon I have at my disposal is *you*."

Ellie braced herself, but she did not close her eyes. The Tinker reached out, his fingertips inching towards her. And then he faltered.

"Ack! Shit!"

Something latched onto his leg, and he tried to kick it away. A white arm gripped his ankle from over the edge of the platform.

"Let go of me, you shit! You already had your chance!"

The mangled corpse of Cassandra, the bride who had leapt off the cliff, rose from below the platform. Her face had been partially eaten by coyotes and her white gown was shredded and dirtied. She brought her other arm up and latched it onto the Tinker's pants.

Now was Ellie's chance. She ran, passing the Tinker, off the platform and towards the woods.

"Don't you try—don't!" The Tinker managed to kick the dead bride off and gave chase after Ellie. He was stopped as he passed a tree by an arm that snaked out and snatched him by his hood. The corpse of Jacob Langley emerged from the tree, hanging from his noose, seizing the Tinker.

"All of you—all of you already made your choice!" The Tinker spat. "What makes you think that you can just stop me now? Huh!"

Ellie stopped and looked. She saw Jacob Langley's decomposing corpse wrapping its arms around the Tinker's neck. From the shadows, the dead girl Ellie had taken the butterfly pendent from emerged. Her face was stained with dried vomit and blood poured from her gashed wrists. She also grabbed the Tinker, trying to get him to stop flailing. The fallen bride had managed to climb up onto the platform, and she staggered towards the Tinker, her bones cracking and grinding, and latched onto him along with the others.

"All of you! Let go of me!" The weight of the forests' dead brought the Tinker to his knees. "You did this to yourselves! All of you knew that you weren't worth a lick of shit!"

A low groaning sound came, dancing on the wind. Ellie saw the visage of the Donneur Vie standing within the forest. Its crown dripped mud and its mouth was wide open, as if it was trying to call to Ellie.

Its voice spoke in her mind: "Run."

Ellie did not hesitate. She fled, and the Tinker's relentless demands for her soul followed her.

The tree branches overhead spread out, and the moonlight poured in, guiding her way through the forest. She made it back to the Butte-de-Tahure trail, and she knew that if she just followed it downwards, she would be at the fork where the Main Trail was. If she went down the Main Trail, then she would be free.

With the moonlight guiding her, she ran through the forest. The spirits of the forests' dead did not disturb her escape. Unafraid, she sprinted, gritting her teeth against the freezing wind on her face. Every nerve, gland and muscle in her body was suddenly filled with life. It kept her going, reminded her that she was alive.

"I'm coming," she gasped.

After passing the fork where she had met the Tinker, she went down the Main Trail. Tears of determination, exhaustion and ferocity ran from her eyes as she passed through the covered bridge, making it to the other side.

"Push," Ellie told herself. "Don't stop!"

Now she was out of the Adrienne Forest, closing in on the parking lot. Through the foliage she saw flashing blue lights—police cruisers.

"I'm here!" Ellie screamed. "I'm right here!"

She leapt over the barrier arm separating the forest from the parking lot and ran into those lights. Within them, she saw the silhouette of a man walking towards her.

"Clancy!" she called.

The silhouette held its arms out. "Ellie!"

She fell into him. Clancy squeezed her. Ellie buried her face into his chest as he ran his fingers through her hair.

"Ellie," he whispered.

"I'm alive," she told him. "I'm still here. I'm alive."

2018

Jayson Robert Ducharme

Thank you for purchasing *Come Forth in Thaw*.

If you enjoyed this book, please consider leaving a review on Amazon. Every review counts and helps the book's ranking and visibility. If you'd like updates on future content, free promotions, giveaways, and more, then subscribe to my newsletter at www.jaysonrobertducharme.com.

J.R.D.

Come Forth in Thaw

Acknowledgements

Writing a book is a solitary endeavor, but it is given its wings by others. I'd like to acknowledge everyone who helped with the launch of this book.

Shawn Connor, Jon Pierce, Justin Rogers, Joe Cabral, C.M. Dotson, Erica Wiggins, Josh Keown, Hayla Richards, Jennifer Brum, Suhasini Sukavashi (willowofwords), Chantale (tal.books), Kia Weathersby, Jennifer Dockery, Tylor James, John Mountain (Books of Blood), Chris Sniadecki, Ashley Jackson, Jacob Ian DeCoursey, Gab Harvey, Jessica (readswithfoxes), Laura (thealc0ve), Alexis (readingwithlexis), Michael R Goodwin, Carla Eliot, Tyler Bloodworth, Christine Laoutaris, Paul Preston, Kristina (nw.reader), Karla Kay, Jennifer Claywood, Todd Young, Kaylie Seed, Melanie Ever Moore, Panayiotis Antoniades (Pan Book Reviews), Nikki Stickney, Heather Miller, Liana Hubert, Kelly LaBouf, Jess Ross (The Bathtub Bookworm), Dylan Raeann, Erin Anthony, Megan Wilcox, Sarah (thebookish_daydreamer), Ashley Upshaw, Christopher McCormick, Haley (between_history_and_horror), Manda (bearpiglovesbooks), Shannon Crescent, Miguel Jorge, Adam Kennedy, Holly Torres, Sam (macmantha), Aiden Merchant, Barbara de Oliveira, Amanda Carvajal, Jeremy Megargee, Adrian Johnson, Paul (man_of_ideas), Ali Ibrahim, Richard Rodriguez, Selena Krivoruchko (beautys.library), Teemu Saarenpaa (forenseek_truecrime_history) and Mers Sumida (Harpies in the Trees)

Come Forth in Thaw

Printed in Great Britain
by Amazon

56556829R00066